www.mascotbooks.com

The Chuck Book: An Interactive ABC Storybook for Everyone

The Chuck Book is not endorsed by Instagram or any of its affiliates. The Instagram handles of the animals featured in this book are located at the bottom of the pages for you and your families to simply find and follow.

WWW.THECHUCKBOOK.COM
For more information, please contact:
Mascot Books
620 Herndon Parkway, Suite 320
Herndon, VA 20170
info@mascotbooks.com

Library of Congress Control Number: 2018905966

CPSIA Code: PRT0618A
ISBN-13: 978-1-64307-118-3

Printed in the United States

IN MEMORY OF OUR DOG BRUCE
AND THE OTHERS WHO ARE PLAYING
TOGETHER ACROSS THE RAINBOW BRIDGE,
YOU'RE ALWAYS IN OUR HEARTS!

THE CHUCK BOOK

AN INTERACTIVE ABC STORYBOOK FOR EVERYONE

STARRING CHUCK THE DUCK & FUR-ENDS!

YOU CAN FIND THE REAL CHUCK AND OTHER CHARACTERS FROM THIS BOOK ON INSTAGRAM!

SEARCH FOR @CHUCK.THE.DUCK   #THECHUCKBOOK

WRITTEN AND ILLUSTRATED BY CODY VANDEZANDE

A is for Archie who approves The Big Apple,
always admiring the alluring old chapel.
Chuck would agree that Archie has it made,
but, "What's that up there, it looks like a parade!"
Oh, that's only Angus, he's approaching alright,
to share his anchovy and tuna delight!

Archie
@approvedbyarchie

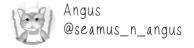
Angus
@seamus_n_angus

B is for Benny and Bruce and Beau.
Boys will be boys, and that's how it goes!
"Let's start a band!" says Chuck to the boys.
"We'll all wear bandanas and call ourselves NOISE!"
Chuck plays the banjo and Benny bangs drums,
Beau rocks the bagpipes, and Bruce just hums.

C is for Claude who's not a cat.
Our clammy new friend claims to chat.
Chuck's friends named Corrie and Chatter
all cackle out loud when they hear a splatter!
A "CROOOOAK" calls out with a curious surprise,
a loud belch releases some crusty old flies!

Corrie
@catchingupwithcorrie

Claude
@tig_n_bai

Chatter (Cheeto)
@instacatgrams

D is for Dexter who's dressed very dapper,
for his date with Delaney who's wearing a flapper!
Chuck pulls up to drive them downtown
in his dusty old clunker that's rusty brown.
They go to a place called Doris and Dean's,
a secret dance club with a dazzling scene!

Dexter
@furdexter

Delaney
@delaney_gram

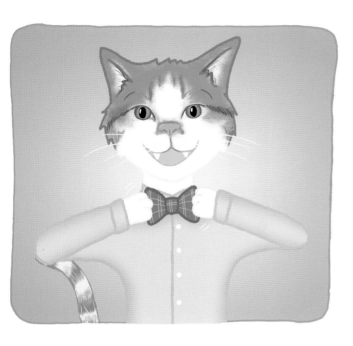

E is for Eevee who's up very early,
excited to eat breakfast with Esteban and squirrelly.
Chuck emerges from the blankets with ease
to find them exploring and chasing the bees!
Elm trees and evergreens surrounding the scene,
embracing the excitement is what it all means!

Eevee
@whiskered_away

Esteban
@estebancat

F is for Frida who has fine fashion.

Flaunting her style is always a passion.

Chuck follows in with a fresh new faux hawk,

and Fritz finds feathers that'll fly on the catwalk!

Flonchy looks fantastic in her long floral gown.

This certainly is the flashiest show in town!

 Frida
@frida_pink_chihuahua

 Fritz
@mookeet75

 Flonchy
@flonchythecat

G is for Gertrude whose garden is growing.

Grapes and gourds are grandly flowing.

Chuck stops by with Gunther and Gertie

to have some tea around six-thirty.

The day grew dark and the garden began to glow,

the gnomes and the fairies all started to show!

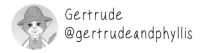 Gertrude
@gertrudeandphyllis

  Gunther & Gertie
@gingerbeautyandherbeasties

H is for Harvey Hedge who's happy to host.
Chuck holds up his glass to give a toast.
"Happy birthday to Hugo!" they all say out loud,
which makes him feel happy to see the crowd.
Hugo is honored to have such good friends,
hugging and laughing, the fun never ends!

Harvey
@miss.harveys.home

Hugo
@gogo.hugo

I is for Ivan whose good friend is Izzy.

She owns Izzy's Ice Cream and it's always so busy!

Iced treats and candies and baked goods galore,

Ivan and Chuck are impressed by the store!

Chuck has an inkling for some indigo ice cream,

and Ivan impatiently inhales his blue icing!

Ivan
@ivan.thecat

Izzy
@blue_eyed_izzy

J is for Jonathon who's joyfully jiving
to the live jazz where music is thriving!
Chuck jumps in on the jamboree of fun
to join the locals and the jovial ones!
Beaded jewels and laughter from all around,
Jingles the jester jokes with the crowd!

 Jonathon
@jonathontheraccoon

 Jingles
@jinglesthecat

K starts the name of a kitty named Knox,

who keeps his kiwis inside a box!

Kohl sips on his kipper fish smoothie,

and Chuck knits a kilt as they watch scary movies!

A loud knock at the door and Kohl kicks out,

the kiwis and knitting go soaring about!

Knox
@meow_york_kitties

Kohl
@kohls_mewsings

Knock!
Knock!
KNOCK!

L is for Lulu who looks like a lion.

Little Lily is dressed in something Hawaiian.

They laugh out loud when Chuck and Lando arrive,

showing up as Mr. Bumble and Mr. Beehive!

Down by the lake the party is lavish,

the costumes are lovely, especially Ms. Radish!

 Lulu
@luluthecatmodel

 Lily
@the.meownsters

 Lando
@landothehusky

M is for Monty who's making his rounds.
Monitoring the magic at the Maplewood Grounds.
The farm is magnificent and managed quite well,
when all of a sudden he hears a loud yell!
It's Chuck and Maddi, they soar from the middle,
riding the sheep while playing the fiddle!

Monty
@monty.at.the.zoo

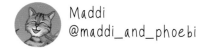
Maddi
@maddi_and_phoebi

N is for Napkins who notices Chuck,
who's ordering nachos at Naranjita's food truck!
They're called Nifty Nachos and built nine feet high,
and if you finish the plate, you win a grand prize!
The rule is that you can share with just one —
they still can't finish but it sure was fun!

 Napkins
@napkinsthecat

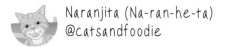 Naranjita (Na-ran-he-ta)
@catsandfoodie

Naranjita's Nifty Nachos

9 ft tall - - - - - - - - - - -

Cheese →

← Sour Cream

Salsa →

← Lettuce

Onion →

← Meat

Chips →

O is for Oscar who sits by the ocean.
He hears an odd and overt commotion.
It's Chuck and Olivia with oodles of gear,
they obviously plan to stay for a year!
Oscar offers some help to his friends,
so they can bask in the sun 'til the day ends.

Oscar + Olivia
@lordoscarmiloragdoll

P is for Pecan who's Chuck's good ol' friend,
pouncing on pillows and playing pretend.
Penny is purring from behind the mirror.
She can't see the party, but can perfectly hear!
Penny's friend Phil helps show her the way,
and they all are pleased with such a fun day!

Pecan
@pecanthenut

Penny
@pennyandwillow

Phil
@phil.verde

Q is for Quincy who's on a quest
to make a quiche, but only the best!
Chuck quickly goes to the grocery store,
where he gets what they need and a little bit more.
Quinn the queen of quiches arrives,
to judge all the dishes and give a grand prize!

R is for Reggie who whistles a song.
Roo and Rainbow are humming along.
They stumble upon a radiant rose path
that leads to a radical red mud bath!
Rainbow runs to jump right in,
but Chuck reaches out with a righteous grin!

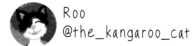
Reggie
@reggie_the_budgie

Roo
@the_kangaroo_cat

Rainbow
@rainbowminipig

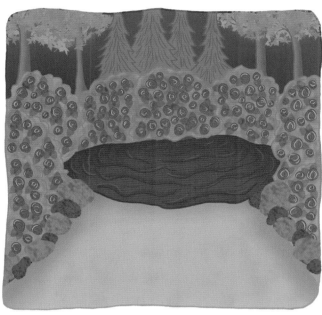

S is for Sophie who's saving the bees.
With help from Stevie, it's such a breeze!
Smedley stops by to drop off some flowers,
so they can plant around the seven foot towers!
The structures are strong and stand up tall,
with spaces for bees, big and small.

Sophie
@sophie_the_model

Stevie (Chuck's sister)
@chuck.the.duck

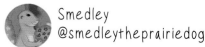
Smedley
@smedleytheprairiedog

T is for Toby who enters a race,
but his tiny tortoise legs can't keep pace!
Tucker and Titan are three times as fast,
but all of a sudden there's a tremendous blast!
It's Tuna and Chuck taking Toby to first,
by slinging him forward with a powerful burst!

Toby
@toby_t_tortoise

Tucker
@tuckerandanniewhitegoldens

Titan
@catventure_bros

Tuna
@therealtunasandwich

U is for Uno who upcycles used junk,

and Ubu who brings a useful blue trunk!

They unite to update Chuck's old tree fort,

by patching up holes and adding support.

Before they could blink, the tree fort grew

into something unique and totally new!

Uno
@cora13cats

Ubu
@ubu_the_cat

V is for Vinny who visits Vermont.
He stops for lunch at a vegan restaurant.
Reading the specials, Vito suggests
the vegetable fritters, they're voted the best!
He sits down by Chuck and admires the view,
the vast landscape has a beautiful hue!

 Vinny
@mrprincevincent

 Vito
@vito_dachshund

W is for Wallace whose whiskers are wild.
He asks wacky Wellington to have them styled.
Willow would like a whimsical new hairdo,
so Chuck brings out the wicked strong hair glue!
Wallace and Willow are pleased with their looks,
this one will surely go down in the books!

 Wallace
@jackandwallace

 Wellington
@wellingtonfloof

 Willow
@itsizzyandwillow

X is for Xena who looks in a mirror.
Everything's reversed but it's perfectly clear!
She can see little Xavier inside of a box,
playing with Chuck, a fox, and an ox!
She steps right through on the count of six
to a magical world full of laughter and tricks!

Xena
@xena_doggy

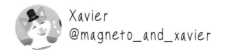
Xavier
@magneto_and_xavier

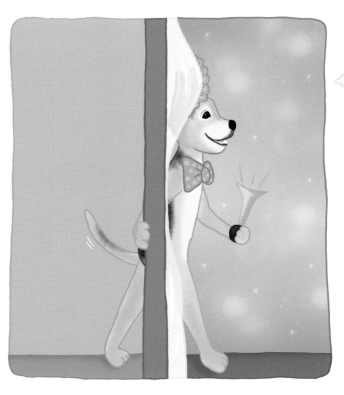

Y is for Yeezy who's in a yoga class.
They're all outside, spread across the grass!
Chuck is the yogi and instructs to exhale,
a "YAAAAAH" yelps out that sounds like a whale!
The whole class turns to see Mr. Yadi,
yodeling out loud while stretching his body!

Yeezy
@yeezycatandco

Yadi
@yadi_cat

Z is for Zeppelin who zigzags around,
Chuck zeroes in once he hears the sound.
"Zow!" yells Zeppelin as Chuck zips past.
Zooming in on the dot to catch it at last!
They both look confused when it disappears.
Zazu's been fooling them all of these years!

Zeppelin
@thiscatzeppelin

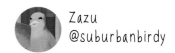
Zazu
@suburbanbirdy

ABOUT CHUCK

CHUCK WAS ADOPTED FROM A FARM IN WISCONSIN AS A KITTEN IN 2007.
HE WAS THE LAST LITTLE GUY IN THE LITTER! IMMEDIATELY FALLING IN LOVE, CODY HAD TO TAKE HIM HOME.
LITTLE DID HE KNOW THAT THIS CUTE BALL OF GINGER FLUFF WOULD GROW UP TO HAVE
QUITE THE PERSONALITY AND WOULD BECOME AN INSTAGRAM CAT-LEBRITY!

CODY DECIDED TO MAKE AN INSTAGRAM ACCOUNT IN LATER YEARS TO POST SOME OF THE
MILLIONS OF PICTURES HE TOOK OF HIM. CODY CHOSE @CHUCK.THE.DUCK
SIMPLY BECAUSE IT RHYMED AND HE IS DEFINITELY A DUCKY CHARACTER!

IN JUST A FEW DAYS HIS FOLLOWING STARTED TO GROW! CODY KNEW THEY WERE ONTO SOMETHING...
WITH HIS COSTUMES, HAIR EXTENSION WIGS, AND CUTE FACE, HOW COULD ANYONE NOT BE
ENTERTAINED BY THIS GOOFY GUY?!

ABOUT CODY

CODY GRADUATED WITH HIS BACHELOR'S DEGREE IN ILLUSTRATION AND DESIGN AND PUBLISHED HIS FIRST CHILDREN'S BOOK, *A GREAT WHITE CHRISTMAS*, IN 2015.

THE CHUCK BOOK IS HIS SECOND SELF-PUBLISHED CHILDREN'S BOOK.

A SPECIAL THANK YOU GOES OUT TO ALL WHO HAVE HELPED MAKE *THE CHUCK BOOK* COME TO LIFE! I'M HUMBLED BY THE AMOUNT OF SUPPORT AND LOVE FROM ALL OF YOU TO HELP ME LIVE MY LIFE DOING WHAT I LOVE TO DO!
- CODY VANDEZANDE